To my son, Grayson who made me a mommy.
I have learned so much about life and love from you.
Thank you for inspiring me and making me a better person.

I love you more!

Written by April Elders

Illustrated by Jennifer Fisher

2023

My mommy had a dream.

It was a really **BIG** one.

It was important and about **LOVE.**

But she needed help with it.

Luckily there were people who could help.

And the day I was born her dream came true.

Some families have a mommy AND a daddy.

Ours just has a mommy.

But we also have me, our kitties, grandma, uncles, aunts, AND lots of great friends too!

We go out and do lots of fun things together.

But sometimes we just stay home together.

We just like to be together.

Mommy and I both love cats.

And the color blue.

I guess we are just meant for each other.

I know I am wanted and loved.

Mommy waited a long time to meet me.

I am so thankful for everyone that helped bring us together.

Not all families are the same.

Some have one parent.

Others have two.

Or maybe three or more.

We are a Mommy Only Family.

All you need is **LOVE** to be a family.

Made in the USA
Middletown, DE
27 July 2025

11315728R00015